LAURA RANKIN

# Fluffy and Baron

Dial Books for Young Readers

DIAL BOOKS FOR YOUNG READERS
A division of Penguin Young Readers Group • Published by The Penguin Group
Penguin Group (USA) Inc., 375 Hudson Street, New York, NY 10014, U.S.A.

Penguin Group (Canada), 90 Eglinton Avenue East, Suite 700, Toronto, Ontario, Canada M4P 2Y3 (a division of Pearson
Penguin Canada Inc.) • Penguin Books Ltd, 80 Strand, London WC2R 0RL, England • Penguin Ireland, 25 St. Stephen's
Green, Dublin 2, Ireland (a division of Penguin Books Ltd) • Penguin Group (Australia), 250 Camberwell Road, Camberwell,
Victoria 3124, Australia (a division of Pearson Australia Group Pty Ltd) • Penguin Books India Pvt Ltd, 11 Community
Centre, Panchsheel Park, New Delhi - 110 017, India • Penguin Group (NZ), Cnr Airborne and Rosedale Roads, Albany,
Auckland 1310, New Zealand (a division of Pearson New Zealand Ltd) • Penguin Books (South Africa) (Pty) Ltd, 24 Sturdee
Avenue, Rosebank, Johannesburg 2196, South Africa • Penguin Books Ltd, Registered Offices: 80 Strand,
London WC2R 0RL, England

Text set in Bitstream Carmina • Manufactured in China on acid-free paper
1  3  5  7  9  10  8  6  4  2

Library of Congress Cataloging-in-Publication Data
Rankin, Laura.
Fluffy and Baron / Laura Rankin.
p.  cm.
Summary: Chronicles the friendship between a duck, Fluffy, and a dog, Baron, from their
first meeting when Fluffy is just a duckling through the time when she has babies of her own.
ISBN 0-8037-2953-7
[1. Dogs—Fiction. 2. Ducks—Fiction. 3. Animals—Infancy—Fiction. 4. Friendship—Fiction.] I. Title.
PZ7+ [E]—dc22    2005003603

*The art was prepared with acrylics and ink on Arches watercolor paper.*

*For Mom and Dad, with love*

One summer day, someone new waddled into Baron's life. Her name was Fluffy.

Baron had to share his food with her . . .

and his water.

At night, she even followed him to his favorite sleeping place.

They became friends.

Every day, the two of them played together.
Baron was good at tag.
Fluffy was great at hide-and-seek.

Both of them were terrific at squirrel-chasing
and fly-snapping.

As the summer passed, Fluffy grew bigger and bigger.

By autumn, she was a full-grown duck.

She and Baron stayed close and warm together all winter long.

Then spring arrived, and three wild ducks landed in the pond. Fluffy watched, waddling back and forth—toward the newcomers and then back to Baron again.

But finally she couldn't resist joining the other ducks. Suddenly Baron had no one to play with him.

When it was time for dinner, Fluffy still hadn't returned.
Baron had to eat alone.

For the next three nights, Fluffy didn't curl up with Baron in their favorite sleeping place.

Then the wild ducks flew away.

Baron tried to play with Fluffy, but she was too busy making a nest. She laid nine eggs in it, then gently settled herself on top and waited for them to hatch.

Four weeks later, there were ducklings!

Fluffy wanted Baron to
be the first one to meet them.
Baron's tail wagged and wagged.
Fluffy's wagged a lot too.

At last it was time to play again. And oh, what fun they all had!

That evening Baron led the way to dinner.

Never had he shared a happier meal.

And after such a busy day, everyone was eager to snuggle in together and fall asleep. Baron felt cozy and warm in his

favorite sleeping place, with nine brand-new friends and best of all, his old friend Fluffy.